AND OTHER MAGICAL STORIES TO READ ALOUD

The Sea-Baby

AND OTHER MAGICAL STORIES TO READ ALOUD

Compiled by Susan Dickinson
Illustrated by Peter Bailey

Collins
An imprint of HarperCollins*Publishers*

First published in Great Britain by Collins in 1996
First published in paperback by Collins in 1997

Collins is an imprint of HarperCollins *Publishers* Ltd
77-85 Fulham Palace Road, Hammersmith, London, W6 8JB

5 7 9 8 6 4

ISBN 0 00 675187 3

Printed and bound in Great Britain by Caledonian
International Book Manufacturing Ltd, Glasgow G64

CONTENTS

THE SEA-BABY 7
Eleanor Farjeon

THE THIEF AND THE MAGIC 19
Margaret Mahy

THE ODD GLOVE 27
Philippa Pearce

THE WONDERFUL CAKE-HORSE 41
Terry Jones

THE KING OF THE CATS 47
Susan Dickinson (ed.)

THE LEGEND OF ALDERLEY 53
Alan Garner

THE OLD WHITE GHOST AND THE
OLD GREY GRANDDAD 59
Dorothy Edwards

A CLOAK FOR AMANITA 69
Adèle Geras

THE THREE SILVER BALLS 81
Ruth Manning-Sanders

LOST – ONE PAIR OF LEGS 95
Joan Aiken

THE GIRL WHO MARRIED A PIXIE 109
Alison Uttley

THE SEA-BABY

Eleanor Farjeon

*T*he stocking-basket was empty. The old
nurse sat with her hands folded in her lap,
and watched the children fall asleep by firelight.
Only one of them kept awake. Mary Matilda
would not go to sleep. She kept on standing up
in her cot and laughing at the old nurse.

"Can't you go to sleep, then? Ah, you're just
my Sea-Baby over again! She never went to
sleep, either, all the time I nursed her. And she
was the very first I ever nursed. Shut your eyes

and listen while I tell about my Sea-Baby."

I couldn't tell you when it happened: it was certainly a long time after the Flood, and I know I was only about ten years old and had never left the Norfolk village on the sea-coast where I was born. My father was a fisherman and a tiller of the land; and my mother kept the house and spun the wool and linen for our clothes. But that tells us nothing, for fathers have provided the food and mothers have kept the house since the beginning of things. So don't go asking any more when it was that I nursed my very first baby.

It happened like this. Our cottage stood near the edge of the cliff, and at high tide the sea came right up to the foot, but at low tide it ran so far back that it seemed almost too far to follow it. People said that once, long ago, the sea had not come in so close, and that the cliff had gone out many miles farther. And on the far end of the cliff had stood another village. But after the Flood all that part of the cliff was drowned under the sea, and the village along with it. And there, said the people, the village still lay far out to sea under the waves; and on stormy nights, they said, you could hear the church bells ringing in the church tower below the water. Ah, don't you start laughing at your old nanny now! We knew it was true, I tell you. And one day something happened to prove it.

A big storm blew up over our part of the land, the biggest storm that any of us could remember, so big that we thought the Flood had come again. The sky was as black as night all day long, and the wind blew so hard that it drove a strong man backwards, and the rain poured down so that you only had to hold a pitcher out of the window for a second and when you took it in it was flowing over, and the thunder growled and crackled so that we had to make signs to each other for talking was no use, and the lightning flashed so bright that my mother could thread her needle by it. That was a storm, that was! My mother was frightened, but my father, who was weather-wise, watched the sky and said from time to time, "I think that'll come out all right."

And so it did. The lightning and thunder flashed and rolled themselves away into the distance, the rain stopped, the wind died down, the sky cleared up for a beautiful evening, and the sun turned all the vast wet sands to a sheet of gold as far as they eye could see. Yes, and farther! For a wonder had happened during the storm. The sea had been driven back so far that it had vanished out of sight and sands were laid bare that no living man or woman had viewed before. And there, far, far across the golden beach lay a tiny village, shining in the setting sun.

Think of our excitement, Mary Matilda! It was the drowned village of long ago, come back to the light of day.

Everybody gathered on the shore to look at it. And suddenly I began to run towards it, and all the other children followed me. At first our parents called, "Come back! Come back! The sea may come rolling in before you can get there." But we were too eager to see the village for ourselves, and in the end the big folk felt the same about it; and they came running after the children across the sands. As we drew nearer the little houses became plainer, looking like blocks of gold in the evening light; and the little streets appeared like golden brooks, and the church spire in the middle was like a point of fire.

For all my little legs, I was the first to reach the village. I had had a start on the others, and could always run fast as a child and never tire. We had long stopped running, of course, for the village was so far out that our breath would not last. But I was still walking rapidly when I reached the village and turned a corner. As I did so, I heard one of the big folk cry, "Oh, look! Yonder lies the sea." I glanced ahead, and did see, on the far horizon beyond the village, the shining line of the sea that had gone so far away. Then I heard another grown-up cry, "Take care! Take care! Who knows when it may begin to roll back again? We have come far, and oh, suppose the sea should overtake us before we can reach home!" Then, peeping round my corner, I saw everybody take fright and turn tail, running as hard as they could across the mile or so of sands they had just crossed. But nobody had noticed me, or thought of me; no doubt my own parents thought I was one of the band of running children, and so they left me alone there, with all the little village to myself.

What a lovely time I had, going into the houses, up and down the streets, and through the church. Everything was left as it had been, and seemed ready for someone to come to; the flowers were blooming in the gardens, the fruit was hanging on the trees, the tables were spread for the next meal, a pot was standing by the kettle on the hearth in one house, and in another there were toys upon the floor. And when I began to go upstairs to the other rooms, I found in every bed someone asleep. Grandmothers and grandfathers, mothers and fathers, young men and young women, boys and girls: all so fast asleep that there was no waking them. And at last, in a little room at the top of a house, I found a baby in a cradle, wide awake.

She was the sweetest baby I had ever seen. Her eyes were as blue as the sea that had covered them so long, her skin as white as the foam, and her little round head as gold as the sands in the evening sunlight. When she saw me she sat up in her cradle and crowed with delight. I knelt down beside her, held out my arms, and she cuddled into them with a little gleeful chuckle. I carried her about the room, dancing her up and down in my arms, calling her my baby, my pretty Sea-Baby, and showing her the things in the room and out of the window. But as we were looking out of the window at a bird's nest in a tree, I seemed to see the shining line of water on the horizon begin to move.

"The sea is coming in!" I thought. "I must hurry back before it catches us." And I flew out of the house with the Sea-Baby in my arms, and ran as hard as I could out of the village, and followed the crowd of golden footsteps on the sand, anxious to get home soon. When I had to pause to get my breath, I ventured to glance over my shoulder, and there behind me lay the little village, still glinting in the sun. On I ran again, and after a while was forced to stop a second time. Once more I glanced behind me, and this time the village was not to be seen; it had disappeared beneath the tide of the sea which was rolling in behind me.

Then how I scampered over the rest of the way! I reached home just as the tiny wavelets, which run in front of the big waves, began to lap my ankles, and I scrambled up the cliff with the Sea-Baby in my arms, and got indoors, panting for breath. Nobody was at home, for as it happened they were all out looking for me. So

I took my baby upstairs, and put her to bed in my own bed, and got her some warm milk. But she turned from the milk, and wouldn't drink it. She only seemed to want to laugh and play with me. So I did for a little while, and then I told her she must go to sleep. But she only laughed some more, and went on playing.

"Shut your eyes, baby," I said to her. "Hush-hush! Hush-hush!" (just as my own mother said to me). But the baby didn't seem to understand, and went on laughing.

Then I said, "You're a very naughty baby," (as my mother sometimes used to say to me). But she didn't mind that either, and just went on laughing. So in the end I had to laugh too, and play with her.

My mother heard us when she came into the house, and she ran up to find me, delighted that I was safe. What was her surprise to find the baby with me! She asked where it had come from, and I told her; and she called my father, and he stood scratching his head, as most men do when they aren't quite sure about a thing.

"I want to keep it for my own, Mother," I said.

"Well, we can't turn it out now it's in," said

my mother. "But you'll have to look after it yourself, mind."

I wanted nothing better! I'd always wanted to nurse things, whether it was a log of wood, or a kitten, or my mother's shawl rolled into a dumpy bundle. And now I had a little live baby of my own to nurse. How I did enjoy myself that week! I did everything for it; dressed and undressed it, washed it, and combed its hair; and played and danced with it, and talked with it and walked with it. And I tried to give it its meals, but it wouldn't eat. And I tried to put it to sleep, but it wouldn't shut its eyes. No, not for anything I could do, though I sang to it, and rocked it, and told it little stories.

It didn't worry me much for I knew no better; but it worried my mother and I heard her say to my father, "There's something queer about that child. I don't know, I'm sure!"

On the seventh night after the storm, I woke up suddenly from my dreams, as I lay in bed with my baby beside me. It was very late; my parents had long gone to bed themselves, and what had wakened me I did not know, for I heard no sound at all. The moon was very bright and filled the square of my windowpane with silver light; and through the air outside I saw something swimming – I thought at first it was a white cloud, but as it reached my open window I saw it was a lady moving along the air as though she were swimming in water. And the strange thing was that her eyes were fast shut; so that as her white arms moved out and in she seemed to be swimming not only in the air, but in her sleep.

She swam straight through my open window to the bedside and there she came to rest, letting her feet down upon the floor like a swimmer setting his feet on the sands under his body. The lady leant over the bed with her shut eyes, and took my wide-awake baby in her arms.

"Hush-hush! Hush-hush!" she said; and the sound of her voice was not like my mother's voice when she said it, but like the waves washing the shore on a still night; such a peaceful sound, the sort of sound that might have been the first sound made in the world, or else the last. You couldn't help wanting to sleep as you heard her say it. I felt my head begin to nod, and as it grew heavier and heavier I noticed that my Sea-Baby's eyelids were beginning to droop too. Before I could see any more

I fell asleep, and when I awoke in the morning my baby had gone.

"Where to, Mary Matilda? Ah, you mustn't ask me that! I only know she must have gone where all babies go when they go to sleep. Go to sleep. Hush-hush! Hush-hush! Go to sleep!"

THE THIEF AND THE MAGIC

Margaret Mahy

There was once a grubby little hut in a wood, and here lived a thief with his mother who had once been a thief too. However, she got stiffness in the joints and creaked so much that it woke up everyone in the houses she was stealing from. Because of this she went into retirement, but she missed the old days. She used to grumble at her son.

"When I was young, thieves were *thieves* – real craftsmen. We worked day and night at our stealing. But nowadays young thieves only think of the money. We were above that. We'd steal *anything*, just for the love of it."

"Yes, Ma," her young thief would say with a yawn. But mind you, this thief was very lazy, and when his mother told him to go out and steal, he'd always make some excuse and stay home in bed.

One day the thief's mother came into the room and said, "We've run out of butter and cheese and money. Hadn't you better do some stealing?"

"Can't we eat turnips instead?" the thief asked, but his mother was determined. The thief knew he'd have to get up and steal something. Also, he was quite a kind-hearted thief and hated to disappoint his old, creaking mother.

"I won't have to go far," he said. "There's that cabin over the hill. Someone's living there now, and no doubt they will have some cheese and butter and money."

The path over the hill was shining and the hill itself was all golden green in the early summer sun. If the thief had been a poet he could have written a poem, but as it was, his head was full of plans for stealing. He hid behind a tree and watched the cabin. The someone who lived there was a raggedy little man. The thief saw him brush his teeth, then clean his boots, and then the raggedy man went out, walking like a shadow right past the tree where the thief was hiding. Then the thief came out and went down to the cottage. The door was not locked – actually it was wide open. Either the little ragged man was too poor to be scared of robbers, or he had a trusting nature. The thief, stealing-bag in hand, looked around the cabin. It was very bare. There were a mop and a broom and a pair of gumboots behind the door and, hanging from nails in the wall, two long scarves – two *very* long scarves, in fact – one blue and one red. There were two boxes and a suitcase. This was all the furniture in the room. The thief opened his stealing-bag and began stealing. He stole a nutmeg grater and a fishslice. He stole bread and cheese and jam too. He stole a calendar because he liked the picture on it.

Then he got a surprise. Something moved in the corner of the room – sat up and scratched itself. The thief had thought it was a sack, old and unravelling, but it was a dog. It looked more like a tattered sack than a dog, however, so it wasn't the thief's fault he had not realized. The dog finished scratching and lay down again, watching the thief with sharp black eyes.

"Good dog," said the thief, but it took all the fun out of his stealing to know someone was watching him. He took a candle in a half-hearted way, put it in his bag, and made for the door.

Then something strange happened. Music began to come into the air – twangling, out-of-tune-sounding music. It rose and fell, chased itself, lost its place and went wandering. Out from behind the door came the mop and the broom dancing a solemn and stiff little dance, bowing and shaking their hair. *Ting-tang-tong* went the twangling music and the mop and broom began to dance in a circle round the thief. The gumboots began to shuffle and then to stamp and then to do a kicking Russian dance in the corner. The thief watched the boots uneasily for a moment. Then he looked back to the mop and the broom. Somehow they had unhooked the two scarves and were doing a scarf dance, swaying and twisting, winding in and out of their own scarves and out of each

other too. The scarves made red-and-blue loops and waves and coils in the shadows of the little hut.

"Ahem," said the thief, clutching his stealing-bag to his chest. "Thank you, I'm sure." He wanted to please the mop and broom but he couldn't clap then, because his hands were full of stealing-bag. He bowed instead, as they pirouetted on their single legs, and then he made for the open door. Then the dog sat up. All at once the mop and broom made a little rush at him. They looped the scarves round and round him until he was more like a blue-and-red cocoon than a man. When he was bound hand and foot and could move no more, they bowed back to him and went to their places behind the door, where they leant themselves against the door, stiff and still. From its corner the dog watched him keenly.

The thief lay and blinked. There was nothing he could do about anything. At least, since the scarves were made of wool, he was very warm, but he could not escape.

After a while there was the sound of rustling feet and the raggedy little man came in at the door. The dog got up and went to meet him, wagging its tail.

"Oh," said the little ragged man in surprise. "A thief." He went down on his knees and began to unknot and unwind the scarves.

"Yes, sir!" said the thief sharply, as soon as he could. "I am a respectable thief, and let me tell you, this is not what I am used to!"

"I'm very sorry," said the raggedy man humbly.

"If I had known you were a magician," the thief went on, "I wouldn't have come here."

"But I'm not a magician," said the raggedy man. "I'm just a tramp called Jumping Bean. It's my dog who is a magician." The dog smiled at the thief and wagged its tail as if it was a wand. "Is this yours?" Jumping Bean asked, picking up the stealing-bag.

"Yes," said the thief. He added sulkily, "I suppose you'll want your things back again."

Jumping Bean peered into the bag. "Only the fishslice," he said. "Not the other things, and we don't use the nutmeg grater. We don't like nutmeg."

The thief was now free.

"Well," he said, "I must say, magician or not, I'd never wish to steal from the house of a finer fellow than yourself. You've been fair – very fair, and I don't mind giving you back your fish-slice."

"Ah well," said Jumping Bean, "I like to help a fellow creature on his way."

So with these words of mutual esteem the thief and the tramp parted. The thief went home to his creaking mother to boast of his stealing. But Jumping Bean and his dog sat down to eat a fine roast duck with orange sauce which the dog magicked up, because, let me tell you, that dog was a *real* magician!

THE ODD GLOVE

Philippa Pearce

One cold, snowy morning a girl called Prue was walking home from the park with her big brother, Charlie. Prue was grumbling and grizzling because her gloves were wet through with melted snow and her hands were cold. She and Charlie had been in a snowball battle with other children in the park.

In a quiet little street with no one about, Prue began crying in earnest. "Everybody can throw snowballs better than me," she sobbed. "And my hands are so cold – so cold!"

"Take your wet gloves off," said Charlie,

"and stick your hands in your pockets. They'll feel warmer there."

So Prue took her gloves off and handed them to Charlie to keep safe for her. They were new gloves, a Christmas present. They weren't really gloves but mittens – each glove was one big bag for Prue's four fingers and a little bag for Prue's thumb. They were knitted in bright red wool with a P for Prue on the back in blue.

Now Prue and Charlie set off home again, with Prue's hands deep in her pockets and not quite so cold. She had stopped crying. All the same, she was still saying, "I wish I could throw snowballs better. I do wish that!"

But neither of them noticed something. One of Prue's red gloves had fallen to the ground while she was taking them off and handing them to Charlie. This right-hand red glove lay there while Prue and Charlie went on home, not realizing. There it lay in the snow, left behind and as good as lost.

Prue and Charlie had nearly reached home before they found out that they had lost a glove.

"We must have dropped it," said Prue, and she was miserable all over again. But Charlie said they would go back at once, by exactly the way they had come, and look for it as they went. They had a good chance of finding it, he said.

So they began walking back, always on the look-out for the red glove. They came to a quiet little street, and Charlie cried, "There it is! On the railings! Somebody found it and stuck it up there for us to see!"

Sure enough there was a red glove on a spike of the railings that ran along the quiet little street. A breeze blew down the street and the fingers of the glove waved in happy greeting to them.

"No," said Prue. "It's not my glove."

But Charlie had set off at a run, and Prue followed close behind. They stopped and stared at the glove.

"I told you," said Prue. "This isn't mine."

"It must be," said Charlie. "It's the same red and it's got your P for Prue on the back. And it's a right-hand glove."

Prue said, "This glove has four separate fingers and one for the thumb. My Christmas glove was just one bag for the fingers and a little bag for the thumb."

Charlie stared and stared. "And yet it's red with your P for Prue on it. I don't understand."

"I do," said Prue. "This glove's come as a special present for me, in place of my ordinary glove." She picked the glove off its iron spike and put it on. It fitted her hand perfectly, and at once warmed it.

"It doesn't match your other glove," said Charlie. "It's an odd glove."

"I don't mind," said Prue. "I like my odd glove. It's a friendly glove. It feels just right. And it makes my hand feel as if it could throw snowballs straight and far. I want us to go to the park again to throw snowballs."

And so they did, that very afternoon. This time Prue could throw snowballs as well as any of the other children and better than some of the children who were older and bigger than she was. "My glove likes throwing snowballs," Prue said. "It just loves it."

Charlie wanted to try wearing the odd glove himself, and Prue lent it to him. But his hand was too big for it; it wouldn't go on. That was disappointing for Charlie. All the same, he didn't mind too much. He shouted to all the other children, "My little sister is champion snowball thrower!"

And so she was.

"My odd glove is a magic glove," Prue said to herself. "I shall always wear it and never lose it."

Prue wore her odd glove whenever she could. She even went to bed with it. She lay in bed with her head on the pillow and her gloved right hand curled up just under her ear. Then she would close her eyes, and after a while she would be sound asleep. "It sends me to sleep with stories," she said to Charlie.

"You mean your odd glove tells you stories?"

"Of course."

"How can a glove tell stories?" Charlie said. "Gloves can't talk."

"Of course gloves can't talk," said Prue. "But this odd glove puts stories straight into my ear without talking."

"What stories?" asked Charlie.

"Wonderful stories," said Prue; but she would never tell exactly what they were. "They're secret," she said.

Meanwhile, the snowballing in the park came to an end because winter was over. Next, the children in the park played football. Prue was no good at football because she was no good at kicking. But, wearing her odd glove, she was very good at throwing and catching. She was extremely good when the children in the park began playing rounders and cricket. She always wore her odd glove to throw the ball and to catch it. When she wore it, the glove made her fingers tingle, and then her whole hand tingled, and there was a strange tingling in her right arm and through her whole body. It was a joyful, eager, determined sort of tingling.

"You could be a champion at cricket," Charlie said to Prue. "A champion bowler, perhaps. You could play for England one day."

"I'd like that," said Prue. "I'd like to play in a Test Match." (She had been watching England against Australia on television.) "I'd like to be playing for the Ashes."

"I don't think women are allowed to play for the Ashes," said Charlie.

"If I got really, really good," said Prue, "perhaps they'd just have to let me in. And I am getting better and better, aren't I?"

"Yes," said Charlie. "You are."

Prue was holding her gloved right hand lovingly against her cheek. "There's just one sad thing, though."

"What is it?" asked Charlie.

But Prue wouldn't tell.

The sad thing was that as Prue was getting older, her hand was growing bigger. Already her hand had to push hard to get into the odd glove. Soon the glove was so tight that it seemed as if it might split.

One summer's day, very sadly, Prue went to the park without her odd glove, to play cricket with the other children. At first she thought that, without her glove, she would be no good at throwing and catching a ball. But, as soon as the game began, she found that her hand – her arm – her whole body – was tingling with the same joy and skill of the throwing and catching. She was as good as ever, and getting better. Her hand had learnt from the odd glove how best to throw a ball and catch it, and her hand was never going to forget. Indeed, with practice and strength it was going to get better and better and better.

So Prue laid her odd glove in the drawer where she kept her most precious things. "There!" she said. "It's a bit dull for you, but you'll be quite safe."

And all that summer Prue played cricket in the park without her glove. And that was just as well, because who plays any kind of ball-game in hot summer weather wearing a woollen glove?

People strolling in the park would sometimes stop to watch the children's cricket. Sometimes someone who knew about cricket would say, "Just look at that little girl! She doesn't just throw the ball; she *bowls* it. Who on earth can have taught her that?" And then, "Some day she could be a first-class bowler."

At bedtime, at home, Prue would take the odd glove out of its drawer. She went to sleep with it held tight in the hand curled under her ear.

After a while there came a change in Prue. She no longer slept well, and when she woke in the mornings she was sad. Sometimes her eyes were red as if she had been crying. One night Charlie was woken by the sound of her sobbing and went to see what the matter was. Prue was sitting up in bed, weeping, with the odd glove held to her. The glove was not on her hand, of course, but she was cuddling it to her, as if to comfort it.

"It's so unhappy," she told Charlie. "It will only tell me unhappy stories nowadays."

"What stories?" asked Charlie.

"I can't tell you," said Prue, weeping afresh. "They make me feel so bad." But, in the end, she told him. The stories were always about prisoners. There were stories about fish caught in rivers and kept in bowls of water without enough room to swim. There were stories about wild birds kept in cages and not allowed to fly free. There were stories about people who had done nothing wrong but who were kept in prisons and could not escape. Sometimes they were treated kindly by their jailers and given good things to eat and drink. Sometimes they were even brought out from their prison cells for a very short time, but they were always put back. They could never escape from their prisons, and they were desperate for freedom.

The stories that the odd glove told Prue made her feel so sad that she did not want to hear any more of them. She began going to bed without the glove. She left it day and night shut up in the drawer where she kept her most precious things. She still played cricket in the park, but her heart was not in the game.

Then one night, in the middle of the night, she was woken, but she did not know why. Perhaps it was by a tiny sound from the chest of

drawers in her bedroom. She saw by the moonlight that the drawer where she kept her
precious things was open just a slit. And out
through that narrow gap something was
squeezing itself.

Something red.

And there was something blue on the red.

It was the odd glove.

The glove squeezed its way out of the drawer
and clambered on to the top of the chest of
drawers. It used its four fingers as legs, and the
thumb was like a head looking from side to side
and deciding which way to go and how to get
there.

From the top of the chest of drawers the odd
glove jumped down to the windowsill, and
there it paused. Through the glass of the
window it could see the garden, and beyond the
garden there was the street, and beyond that lay
the whole world in which one could be free.

The window was open because of the warm
summer night, but only at the top. There was
plenty of room there for a glove to get out, but
it would have to reach the top first.

Prue saw the odd glove begin to climb up the
window towards the gap at the top. It climbed

on its four fingers up the glass, but the fingers could not get a proper grip on the smooth glass. Again and again they slipped, and then the glove would fall right down on to the windowsill and lie there. And then start all over again.

Every time the odd glove started to climb again, it climbed more slowly. Every time it fell, it had to rest longer before trying again. At last it was so exhausted that it lay on the windowsill, not climbing any more, not even moving.

Prue got out of bed and fetched the odd glove, carrying it tenderly. She lay down again with the glove in her hand and under her ear on the pillow. Then the odd glove told her the saddest story it had ever told. It told her of a prisoner who thought of a way to escape from his prison. He escaped through the door of his prison cell; he escaped through door after inner door of his prison, until he came to the outermost door of all. But he found, to his despair, that he could not escape through that door.

He lay exhausted inside the last door of his prison, and there his jailers found him. They carried him back to his prison cell and shut him in again. There he must remain, they said.

Whether the odd glove told her the whole story, or whether she dreamt the end of it, Prue never knew. She woke up in the morning, remembering and grieving and with a great determination.

She put the odd glove in the pocket of her summer dress, and asked Charlie to come with her; and he did.

She led the way to the quiet little street with the iron railings. She took the odd glove from her pocket and put it up on one of the spikes of the railings. "There!" she said. "Now you are where you need to be."

Then she and Charlie went to the end of the street and just round the corner, out of sight. They counted to twenty. While they counted, nobody went into the street, nobody came out of it, and there were no sounds of footsteps on the pavement or in the road.

After they had counted to twenty, they went back to look down the little street. And there, plain to be seen, was a red glove with a blue P for Prue sticking up on one of the spikes of the railings.

"Oh, dear," said Charlie. "The odd glove's still there. Your idea didn't work."

"Yes, it did!" cried Prue, and she ran down the street and pulled the red and blue glove off its spike. "Look! This glove doesn't have four fingers and a thumb, as the odd glove had. It has just a thumb and a bag for four fingers. It's my old glove that I once had as a Christmas present."

"It's a swap," Charlie said wonderingly. "And there's no explanation? No goodbye to you? No message at all?"

"No message," said Prue. "Nothing. But it's all all right. We can go to the park now and play cricket. Oh, hurry!"

That is the end of the story, except for one thing. If there is ever a young woman playing cricket for England when England is playing Australia for the Ashes, her name will be Prue, and she will be the very best bowler there has ever been.

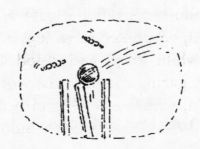

THE WONDERFUL CAKE-HORSE

Terry Jones

A man once made a cake shaped like a horse. That night a shooting star flew over the house and a spark happened to fall on the cake-horse. Well, the cake-horse lay there for a few moments. Then it gave a snort. Then it whinnied, scrambled to its legs and shook its mane of white icing, and stood there in the moonlight, gazing round at the world.

The man, who was asleep in bed, heard the noise and looked out of the window, and saw his cake-horse running around the garden, bucking and snorting, just as if it had been a real wild horse.

"Hey! Cake-horse!" cried the man. "What are you doing?"

"Aren't I a fine horse!" cried the cake-horse. "You can ride me if you like."

But the man said, "You've got no horseshoes and you've got no saddle, and you're only made of cake!"

The cake-horse snorted and bucked and kicked the air, and galloped across the garden, and leapt clean over the gate, and disappeared into the night.

The next morning the cake-horse arrived in the nearby town, and went to the blacksmith and said, "Blacksmith, make me some good horseshoes, for my feet are only made of cake."

But the blacksmith said, "How will you pay me?"

And the cake-horse answered, "If you make me some horseshoes, I'll be your friend."

But the blacksmith shook his head. "I don't need friends like that!" he said.

So the cake-horse galloped to the saddler, and

said, "Saddler! Make me a saddle of the best leather – one that will go with my icing-sugar mane!"

But the saddler said, "If I make you a saddle, how will you pay me?"

"I'll be your friend," said the cake-horse.

"I don't need friends like that!" said the saddler, and shook his head.

The cake-horse snorted and bucked and kicked its legs in the air and said, "Why doesn't anyone want to be my friend? I'll go and join the wild horses!" And he galloped out of the town and off to the moors where the wild horses roamed.

But when he saw the other wild horses, they were all so big and wild that he was afraid they would trample him to crumbs without even noticing he was there.

Just then he came upon a mouse who was groaning to himself under a stone.

"What's the matter with you?" asked the cake-horse.

"Oh," said the mouse, "I ran away from my home in the town, and came up here where there is nothing to eat, and now I'm dying of hunger and too weak to get back."

The cake-horse felt very sorry for the mouse, so it said, "Here you are! You can nibble a bit of me, if you like, for I'm made of cake."

"That's most kind of you," said the mouse, and he ate a little of the cake-horse's tail, and a little of his icing-sugar mane. "Now I feel much better."

Then the cake-horse said, "If only I had a saddle and some horseshoes, I could carry you back to town."

"I'll make you them," said the mouse, and he made four little horseshoes out of acorn cups, and a saddle out of beetle-shells, and he got up on the cake-horse's back and rode him back to town.

And there they remained the best of friends for the rest of their lives.

THE KING OF
THE CATS

retold by Susan Dickinson

*O*ne dark winter evening the village grave-digger's wife was sitting beside the fire with her black cat, Old Tom, on her lap. She was waiting for her husband to come home and couldn't think why he was so late. It was long after dark and nobody would be digging graves at this hour of the night.

Suddenly the door opened and in he rushed, calling out in a wild sort of way, "Who's Tom Tildrum?" His cap was off and his hair was blown all over the place. "Who's Tom Tildrum?" he repeated.

"Whatever's the matter?" said his wife. And the cat sat up on her lap and stared at his master. "Why do you want to know who Tom Tildrum is?"

"Oh, I've had such an adventure," said the grave-digger. "I was digging away at old Mr Finlayson's grave, and the ground was so hard I sat down for a moment. I suppose I must have fallen asleep for the next thing I heard was a cat's miaow."

"*Miaow!*" said Old Tom.

"Yes. It was just like that! I peeped over the edge of the grave, and what do you think I saw?"

"I haven't any idea at all," said his wife.

"Why, there were nine black cats, just like our Tom here, and each one had a white spot on its chest. And what do you suppose they were doing? They were processing through the graveyard, carrying a small coffin covered with a velvet cloth. And on top of the cloth was a tiny golden coronet. At every third step they all cried out together: *Miaow.*"

"*Miaow!*" said Old Tom again.

"Yes, it was exactly like that," said the grave-digger. "They came towards me with their eyes shining. There were eight of them carrying the coffin and the biggest cat walked in front, looking just like – but look at our Tom, how he's staring at me! You would think he was listening to every word!"

"Go on, go on," said his wife. "What happened? Never mind our Old Tom."

"Well, as I was saying, they came slowly towards me, and at every third step they cried *Miaow*!"

"*Miaow*!" said Old Tom again.

"Well, they came right up to me and stopped just at old Mr Finlayson's grave. They all stood quite still and looked at me. But look, look at Old Tom! He's listening to every word!"

"Oh, do go on," said his wife. "Never mind Old Tom."

"Oh yes. Well, the one that was walking in front came forward and staring hard at me, said to me in a squeaky sort of voice – yes, he actually *spoke* to me, 'Tell Tom Tildrum that Tim Toldrum is dead.' But how can I tell Tom Tildrum that Tim Toldrum is dead if I don't know who Tom Tildrum is?"

"Look at Old Tom! Look at Old Tom!" screamed his wife. For Old Tom had jumped off her lap and was standing before the fire, staring at the grave-digger, his fur rising and his head held high.

"What?" he shrieked – "Tim Toldrum dead? Then *I'm* the King o' the Cats!" And he rushed up the chimney and they never saw him again.

THE LEGEND OF ALDERLEY

Alan Garner

At dawn one still October day in the long ago of the world, across the hill of Alderley, a farmer from Mobberley was riding to Macclesfield fair.

The morning was dull, but mild; light mists bedimmed his way; the woods were hushed; the day promised fine. The farmer was in good spirits, and he let his horse, a milk-white mare, set her own pace, for he wanted her to arrive fresh for the market. A rich man would walk

back to Mobberley that night.

So, his mind in the town while he was yet on the hill, the farmer drew near to the place known as Thieves' Hole. And there the horse stood still and would answer to neither spur nor rein. The spur and rein she understood, and her master's stern command, but the eyes that held her were stronger than all of these.

In the middle of the path, where surely there had been no one, was an old man, tall, with long hair and beard. "You go to sell this mare," he said. "I come here to buy. What is your price?"

But the farmer wished to sell only at the market, where he would have the choice of many offers, so he rudely bade the stranger quit the path and let him through, for if he stayed longer he would be late to the fair.

"Then go your way," said the old man. "None will buy. And I shall await you here at sunset."

The next moment he was gone, and the farmer could not tell how or where.

The day was warm, and the tavern cool, and all who saw the mare agreed that she was a splendid animal, the pride of Cheshire, a queen among horses; and everyone said that there was no finer beast in the town that day. But no one offered to buy. A weary, sour-eyed farmer rode up out of Macclesfield as the sky reddened the west.

At Thieves' Hole the mare would not budge: the stranger was there.

Thinking any price now better than none, the farmer agreed to sell. "How much will you give?" he said.

"Enough. Now come with me."

By Seven Firs and Goldenstone they went, to Stormy Point and Saddlebole. And they halted before a great rock imbedded in the hillside. The old man lifted his staff and lightly touched the rock, and it split with the noise of thunder.

At this, the farmer toppled from his plunging horse and, on his knees, begged the other to have mercy on him and let him go his way unharmed. The horse should stay; he did not want her. Only spare his life, that was enough.

The wizard, for such he was, commanded the farmer to rise. "I promise you safe conduct," he said. "Do not be afraid; for living wonders you shall see here."

Beyond the rock stood a pair of iron gates.

These the wizard opened, and took the farmer and his horse down a narrow tunnel deep into the hill. A light, subdued but beautiful, marked their way. The passage ended and they stepped into a cave, and there a wondrous sight met the farmer's eyes – a hundred and forty knights in silver armour, and by the side of all but one a milk-white mare.

"Here they lie in enchanted sleep," said the wizard, "until a day will come – and come it will – when England shall be in direst peril, and England's mothers weep. Then out from the hill these must ride and, in a battle thrice lost, thrice won, upon the plain, drive the enemy into the sea."

The farmer, dumb with awe, turned with the wizard into a further cavern, and here mounds of gold and silver and precious stones lay strewn along the ground.

"Take what you can carry in payment for the horse."

And when the farmer had crammed his pockets (ample as his lands!), his shirt, and his fists with jewels, the wizard hurried him up the long tunnel and thrust him out of the gates. The farmer stumbled, the thunder rolled, he looked, and there was only the bare rock face above him. He was alone on the hill, near Stormy Point. The broad full moon was up, and it was night.

And although in later years he tried to find the place, neither he nor any after him ever saw the iron gates again. Nell Beck swore she saw them once, but she was said to be mad, and when she died they buried her under a hollow bank near Brindlow wood in the field that bears her name to this day.

THE OLD WHITE GHOST
AND THE
OLD GREY GRANDDAD

Dorothy Edwards

*T*here was once an old white ghost who
lived behind a water pipe in an old-fashioned scullery in an old, old house. In this
scullery was a big stone sink and a great copper
boiler for washing clothes.

For many years this old white ghost haunted
the scullery. He made terrible noises in the
water pipes, and after dark, when someone
came downstairs to iron the clothes by candle-

light, he would slip inside the clothes basket and ruffle the washing and then shoot up suddenly in a sheet, or creep across the floor in an old black sock.

Some nights he would blow feathers from the pillowslips in front of the candle to make strange shadows on the wall; and sometimes – sometimes he would drip a cold-water drop on the neck of the person who was ironing. One cold drop. Aaah!

And then he'd blow the candle out. Oooh!

People hated his tricks. They became very frightened. Soon they refused to go into the scullery at all.

They stopped using it for washing, and over the years it got filled up with all the things no one wanted to throw away.

At last a very large family came to live in that old house. There was a father and mother and their seven children and an old grey granddad. Now there was a battered pram and an old push-bike, an old clothes wringer with wooden rollers for crushing water out of the washing, and several old tubs, and a great bundle of comics on the scullery floor. In the stone sink stood a pile of old gramophone records and an old-fashioned gramophone with a tin horn and a handle to wind it up. Perched on top of the copper was an old basket chair. And over and under and between all these things were broken toys and rags and rubbish.

The mother took all her washing to the launderette up the road, and as all her family wore drip-dry clothes, no ironing was needed. So nobody ever went into the scullery.

All these things that nobody wanted got dustier and dustier, under a great grey cobweb blanket.

At night the old white ghost came out from behind the water pipe and made ghostly noises. He moaned and sighed until the cobwebs rocked and shivered and the basket chair creaked. But there was no one to hear him. No one to tremble with fear or run away shrieking. "I might as well not bother," the old white ghost said mournfully.

One reason why no one heard him was because there were so many noises in the house anyway. The family never stopped making noises of one kind or another: shouting, hammering, sawing, sewing-machining, vacuuming, and quarrelling. And the radio, TV, and hi-fi were always switched on, all at the same time.

Only the old grey granddad was quiet. He sat in a chair in the corner of the sitting room with his hands over his ears to keep out the din.

One day this old grey granddad felt he couldn't stand the racket any longer, so he got out of his chair and began to prowl about the house. Every room was filled with people, their things, and their noise!

"If only I could find somewhere quiet," the poor old man said. "If only I could find a quiet place for myself."

At last he crept down the kitchen steps and found himself in the scullery. The spiders had woven so many webs that only a dim light crept through the window, but the old man peered around in the gloom and took a fancy to what he saw.

"Why," he said, "I could make myself a snug little place down here. I could get them upstairs to help me clear out the rubbish and, with a lick of whitewash here and a dab of paint there, it would come up a treat!

"After all," said the old grey granddad, "I more than pay my way so they owe me something!"

And all the time he stood there talking to

himself, the old white ghost watched him from behind the water pipe in the corner. The old white ghost was interested, but he didn't show himself, he just waited and bided his time.

The old grey granddad went back upstairs and he began to shout – louder than the loudest child to make himself heard.

"I pay my way," he yelled, "so I've got my rights. I want that scullery downstairs for my own private place and I'd thank you all to help me clear it out and make it homelike."

And because his family were very fond of him, and because they knew he had justice on his side, they all stopped their hammering, banging, sawing, machining, shouting and making all the other noises, and got together to clear out the old-fashioned scullery.

What a time they had – carrying all the old things out into the yard and stacking them up by the dustbins!

Sometimes the old grey granddad would shout, "Not that! I could do with that!"

In that way he saved the basket chair for himself. He got the two youngest children scrubbing it clean, and the mother upstairs looking out a cushion for it. "I always liked to sit

in a basket chair," the old grey granddad said.

He found an old folding table behind the wringer, and enough planks of wood to make himself some shelves; as for the old gramophone with the tin horn – he went mad with joy when that turned up, and he looked at the pile of records. "All those old songs – all those old bands!" he said. "They don't make music like that nowadays. I can listen to my heart's content."

And when they began to clear out the bundles of old comics he said, "Weary Willie and Tired Tim! Why that takes me back to my boyhood! They'll be just the thing for me to read when I'm sitting in my basket chair with my table at my elbow."

And all this time the old white ghost made never a sound nor a movement, he just watched from behind the water pipe. He watched while they cleared the scullery. He watched while they whitewashed and painted and hung shelves. He watched while the father laid a carpet that the mother had found in a second-hand shop. He watched and waited until at last the old grey granddad was alone in his nice new quarters; until he was sitting in his basket chair with his pile of old comics on the table and the freshly oiled gramophone and the well-dusted records to hand in the nicely scrubbed sink.

He waited till the old man had switched on the electric lamp that the father had wired for him, and spread out his toes to the electric fire the eldest grandson had fixed in place of the old copper-fire, and reached for the first copy of *Chips* before "Uuuggh – Ah-h-h-h," he said in the water pipe. "Uh, uh, uh, uh!"

He looked hard at the old grey granddad, but the old man didn't stir. After all the family racket he'd put up with for so long, he wasn't to be upset by ghostly water pipes. Instead, he smiled sweetly, and leaning forward, he wound the handle of the gramophone, and the scullery was full of the gay and scratchy sound of a long-ago band of the Grenadier Guards. It was as if the ghosts of the old dead bandsmen filled the little warm scullery as they listened to their music. The old granddad welcomed them with pleasure.

The old white ghost was puzzled.

Presently, however, he grew bold again, and he began to rustle the pile of comics, but the old grey granddad didn't seem to mind a bit. He just picked up a big flatiron that he was using for a doorstop and put it on top of the pile. "Draughts," he said.

The old white ghost remembered his trick with the water and loosed a drop on the old granddad's neck. "Condensation," said that happy old man. "It's the old pipes warming up."

The old white ghost tried to blow out the light as he'd blown out candles in the old haunting days. But the electric bulb never flickered, and the old grey granddad went on to read *Comic Cuts*.

The old white ghost was baffled. He began to moan from sheer despair. "I want to haunt you," he said. "Please let me frighten you."

The old grey granddad looked up over his spectacles and saw the flickering outline of the old white ghost. "It's no good," he said, "I know all about you. Everyone knows about you. You think you're a ghastly spectre and so did a lot of other people. I know you're just draught, and air-locks in the pipes, and condensation – I know you can be mice or rats or imagination, so don't ask me to be afraid of you.

"I'll tell you what," said the old grey grand-dad, "there's an old stool over in the corner. I'll bring it up near to the fire here, and you can sit yourself down beside me and listen to the music. You can take a peek over my shoulder at these comics, they're good for a laugh any time. In that way I won't worry you and you won't worry me."

And that's just what the old white ghost did. He perched himself on the stool and listened to the long-dead voices of comic singers and mournful singers, and the long-lost strains of forgotten bands. Sometimes he took a peek over the old granddad's shoulder and they laughed together over old jokes.

And if sometimes the old white ghost got up from his stool and made ghostly noises in the pipes, or moaned and wailed for old times' sake, the old grey granddad only said, "Ah – but if it's real noise you're after – that lot upstairs can beat you hollow!"

A CLOAK FOR AMANITA

Adèle Geras

*O*ne blue summer evening, a tall figure perched on a walking stick flew in through Aunt Pinny's window and landed daintily on the rug. Aunt Pinny was busy making a wedding dress. She put down her sewing and said in an unsurprised voice, "Good evening, madam. Is there anything I can do to help you?"

"My name," said the stranger, "is Amanita Deathcap, and this –" she scrabbled around in a flood of black skirts and produced a fat, black, mangy cat "– is Fungus, my cat."

"Charmed," said Aunt Pinny. "I don't think I've ever had the pleasure of meeting a witch before. Please sit down. May I offer you a glass of sherry?"

"I should prefer a long blood and tonic," said Amanita wearily. "But sherry will do nicely, thank you. Blood is such a luxury these days, don't you find?"

"I believe they use most of it in hospitals," said Aunt Pinny mildly, putting a glass into Amanita's pale hand. "For transfusions."

"My dear, don't mention such words to me. They turn me quite weak."

Aunt Pinny was enjoying her first visit from a witch. Amanita now seemed well-settled on the sofa, sipping her sherry. Still, witches are unreliable and Aunt Pinny had no intention of letting Amanita fly away on her walking stick before she had had a long and interesting chat. So she said, "I see you do not travel on a broomstick. I always thought . . ."

"My broomstick is being serviced at the moment," said Amanita. "Such a nuisance. This belongs to my daughter. She calls it a Mini. It lacks the elegance of my broomstick, and the speed, but it *is* very convenient for parking. And it uses remarkably little fuel: forty miles to the teaspoon."

"Indeed," said Aunt Pinny. "Teaspoon of what, may I ask? I regret I am so ignorant of modern technology."

"Stardust," replied Amanita. "High octane stardust. One day, perhaps, I shall be wealthy enough to afford a Hoover."

"A Hoover?" Aunt Pinny took a hasty sip of her sherry. "You mean a vacuum cleaner?"

"Oh, my dear!" Amanita leant forward, and Aunt Pinny caught the smell of bitter almonds drifting from her dress. "The very latest in power and performance! But what a price! Don't ask, my dear, simply don't ask! I'm working on a spell that will win me £50,000 on the Premium Bonds but, so far, the computer they use has me totally baffled. Mathematics was always my weakest subject."

"More sherry?" Aunt Pinny rose to refill the glasses.

"How kind," sighed Amanita, holding out her glass in a bony hand. Fungus, the cat, began to prowl discontentedly round the room. "And may I trouble you for a little something for my cat?"

"Certainly," said Aunt Pinny. "Milk? Or Jellymarrow Bouncimogs? Or some fresh liver?"

"I suppose bats would be difficult? Or lightly toasted frogs?"

"I'm afraid so," said Aunt Pinny.

"Then liver would be best."

Fungus followed Aunt Pinny into the kitchen. When she returned to the living room, Aunt Pinny told Amanita, "I have been having a most interesting talk with Fungus."

"To tell you the truth," said Amanita, in a graveyard whisper, "he's a *teensy-weensy* bit of a bore. Pompous, you know. But he has his uses."

"Now," said Aunt Pinny, "may I ask why you have come to see me?"

"Cracked skulls and nailparings! Such a scatterbrain I'm becoming. It's this sherry. It's gone to my head." Amanita giggled hoarsely. "You are a dressmaker, are you not?"

"Yes, I am."

"That is why I've come. I need a new evening cloak. Nothing ordinary, mind you. Something with dash, flair, verve and style. Something spectacular. Something that will dazzle and amaze. I wish to wear it at the Necromancers, Sorcerers, and Allied Magicworkers Annual Dinner and Dance. Now," she breathed, "what do you suggest?"

"There is not," (Aunt Pinny chose her words carefully), "very much one can *do* with a cloak when it comes to styling. A cloak, after all, is cloak-shaped, however you hang it about with ruffles over the shoulders or at the hem. A dramatic effect is generally achieved by lining the cloak in contrasting material. I think what we must try for is novelty of fabric. Something with richness, dignity and sparkle. A fine material *makes* the garment, I always say."

"I quite agree. Nothing ruins an effect more than shoddy cloth. I *deplore* the coming of cheap imports and," she lowered her voice and hissed through greenish teeth, "MAN-MADE FIBRES!"

"I have here," said Aunt Pinny, going to the sideboard, "a box of samples. Perhaps together we can find one that we like for you. Then I shall take your measurements, and tomorrow I can buy the material and make a start in time for a fitting on – say – Tuesday. Will that suit you, madam?"

"Perfectly admirable. Hunky-dory. Delightful," said Amanita. "I need the cloak in a fortnight. Simply oodles of time."

And so they sat on the sofa together, although Aunt Pinny took care that their heads should not touch. There was, about Amanita's waving hair, a suspicion of dirt, the merest hint of lice lurking and fleas flitting. They tossed onto the rug swatches of velvets, brocades and taffetas. They fingered and felt. They held some pieces up to the light, and draped others over their knees. From time to time, Amanita said, "How does this look?" and Aunt Pinny answered, "It doesn't bring out the marvellous yellow in your eyes," or, "Someone of your height should avoid fussy patterns," or simply, "Not quite you, madam, I think." They found nothing suitable. Gloom filled the room.

Fungus pushed a pattern book off the chair with one paw, and said, to no one in particular, "Dear me, at my age, to be fool enough to go shopping with a woman . . . A slight snooze, I think, is called for." He fell asleep, curled up like an ordinary cat.

Then they found it.

"Ooh," said Amanita, "I really think . . ."

"Yes, yes, I do agree," said Aunt Pinny, holding the material up to Amanita's face. "It's perfect. It's the very thing. It's YOU!"

"I think," said Amanita, "that this calls for more sherry."

They raised their glasses in a toast. Amanita spoke, "I give you the wickedest, most devilishly gorgeous piece of cloth in the world." As they drank, they gazed upon the treasure they had found. Satin. Blood-red satin. Not only the colour of blood, but the slippery, slithery, silken texture of blood.

"Please stand up, madam," said Aunt Pinny, "and I will take your measurements."

As she was writing these down in a note-book, she said, "What shall we use for a lining? It will be difficult to find a suitably splendid contrast for that, I fear."

Amanita looked sulkily out of the window at the night sky; the thick, dark blue, star-spotted sky. Opulent, velvety. She leapt to her feet. "The night sky! That's it! How too, too magnificent it looks!"

Aunt Pinny was astonished. "It's lovely," she said, "but I think we must return to the problem of the lining."

"It *is* the lining!" Amanita was almost dancing on the windowsill by now. "The night sky will be my lining. I shall snip off as much as we need. You'll have to tell me how much you want, of course, and lend me your tape measure, and I'll zip up in my Mini and cut as much as necessary. Ha! That'll be one in the eye for Hecate and her tatty cronies. Ha!"

"Won't they miss the bit you snip off?" Aunt Pinny asked doubtfully. "I mean, won't it leave a hole?"

"Well, yes, I suppose it will." Amanita agreed. "But, really, there is so *much* of the sky, don't you think? No one could possibly object to my having a few metres, surely?"

"I suppose not," Aunt Pinny sighed, but she did feel a little nervous about the whole scheme. Amanita picked up her walking stick and poked Fungus gently.

"Arise, old fellow. We're going on a mission."

"Your mission is ill-timed," yawned Fungus. "They always are."

"Come," said Amanita, as she tucked Aunt Pinny's tape measure into a buried pocket. "Goodbye, and thank you so much, my dear. I shall return." She climbed onto the walking stick and threw herself out of the window. Aunt Pinny watched as Amanita's shadow became smaller and smaller, and finally disappeared.

"An unusual evening," she said to herself, and took the glasses out to the kitchen. She washed them and dried them, and washed Fungus's plate and smiled.

"A talking cat? A witch who wants a cloak lined with the night sky? Maybe I'm dreaming." Aunt Pinny went to bed.

The next day, Aunt Pinny went to the little shop that stocked all her materials and bought several metres of blood-red satin, just in case. In the sunlight, with the cars and buses rumbling past, last night seemed more dreamlike than ever. She walked back to the house and stood on the doorstep for a while, feeling in her handbag for the key. Suddenly the door was opened from the inside and there was Amanita.

"Little me again!" she said. "Come in and see what I've got!"

Aunt Pinny hung her hat and coat up in the hall and went into the living room. Her mouth dropped open. Her hands trembled. She sat down very quickly indeed. There, spread rippling over the sofa, was the dark blue, velvety sky, studded and spangled and winking with stars, millions and millions of stars.

"Well," said Aunt Pinny, letting out the breath

she had been holding since she came into the room. "I suppose I had better start cutting out."

Aunt Pinny draped and pinned, pinned and draped. Amanita pirouetted in front of the mirror like a young girl. She left at four o'clock, promising to return for her first fitting on Tuesday.

On Tuesday evening, Amanita flitted in through the window. "Coo-ee!" she chuckled. "Where are you? Yoo-hoo! Don't hide away now!"

"I'm over here," said Aunt Pinny.

"Bat's blood and tombstones, you gave me a fright! Why are you standing over there in the dark? What's the matter? Where's the cloak?"

"I'm afraid," said Aunt Pinny softly, coming into the light, "that something has happened. Something dreadful."

"Show me," said Amanita in a voice of death.

Aunt Pinny pulled a cardboard box from under the sideboard. She opened it, and took out metres and metres of navy-blue cloth. Plain, ordinary navy-blue cloth. Not a star on it. No shine to it. Nothing.

"As I cut it," Aunt Pinny whispered, "the stars faded, the whole glory of it vanished, and here's what we're left with: navy-blue gaberdine. Thick, school skirt stuff. No earthly use at all. I am *so* sorry. We'll have to think again."

Amanita flopped onto the sofa and sighed: "Oh well. Back to the drawing board. I shall have to cut some more, that's all. The sky above London is of very poor quality. All those orange lights, I shouldn't wonder. I think I'll try the sky above the Amazon jungle." She jumped onto her stick. "I shall borrow a Hoover from one of my rich friends and be back in two days. You may make that rubbish into curtains, for all I care. Farewell." Amanita was gone.

Aunt Pinny waited a week. Then a month. Then a year. She put the blood-red satin away in a cupboard, just in case Amanita ever returned. She never did, but Aunt Pinny could not bring herself to use the material. She made the gaberdine into sensible school-uniform skirts for several young ladies, who never realized that they were wearing pieces of the sky.

THE THREE SILVER BALLS

Ruth Manning-Sanders

A poor man and his wife had three little girls. And the man fell ill. His wife cooked him this, and she cooked him that; but no, he couldn't fancy anything except a drop of cabbage soup. Well, the wife hadn't any cabbages, but she knew where there were some. So she said to the eldest little girl, "Go to the goblin's house, and ask him for a few cabbage leaves from his garden. Hurry now!"

The little girl took a little basket and set off.

She came to the goblin's house and knocked, but she couldn't make anyone hear. So she wandered round the garden, looking for the goblin. She couldn't find him, but she saw rows and rows of cabbage plants, and she thought, "Surely he won't mind my picking a few leaves." So she picked a few leaves, and then a few more.

Well, she had nearly filled her little basket when she heard the goblin calling from the house. "What are you doing down there?"

And the little girl answered, "My mamma sent me to get a few cabbage leaves because my papa is ill and can fancy nothing but a drop of cabbage soup."

"Come up here!" called the goblin.

"No, no," said the little girl; "my mamma will scold me if I don't hurry home."

"Come up here!" called the goblin again. "I will give you a present to take home."

So the little girl left her little basket in the garden and went up into the house. And the goblin gave her a silver ball.

"And now you are here," said he, "you may as well look through the house. I have many pretty things, and you may open all the doors and go into all the rooms; but the door at the top of the winding staircase, that door you may not open."

Then the goblin went away, and the little girl began to look through the house. She opened one door after another, and she saw a lot of pretty things, but she didn't linger very long looking at them because she knew she ought to go home with the cabbage leaves. So she came down into the hall again, and was just about to go out of the house when she caught sight of the little winding staircase, and the door at the top of it.

"What can be inside that door?" she said to herself. And since the goblin wasn't anywhere to be seen, she thought she would just take a quick peep inside that door and then go home.

So she ran quickly up the little winding staircase, and opened the door at the top.

Bah! There wasn't a room at all behind that door, there was only a smelly old cupboard. And the floor of the cupboard was all wet and muddy, because it was the mouth of a deep, slimy pit. The little girl backed quickly out of the cupboard, but the door was stiff on its hinges and she couldn't manage to shut it easily.

So she put both her hands to the door latch to pull it to, and in so doing she dropped her ball on the wet, muddy floor.

Oh, oh! Now the pretty silver ball was all dirty!

The little girl picked it up and tried to rub it clean on her apron, but the more she rubbed it, the dirtier it got. So, after having managed at last to slam the cupboard door, she put the ball in her pocket and ran down the winding staircase.

And there was the goblin waiting for her by the front door.

"Where's your silver ball?" said he.

The little girl took the ball out of her pocket and showed it to him.

"Ah, you dirty, disobedient child!" cried the goblin. And he took her by the hair, dragged her up the winding staircase (for though he was very small, he was very strong), wrenched open the cupboard door, and threw the little girl, head first, down into the deep, slimy pit.

Well, of course, the little girl didn't get home with the cabbage leaves; and there was the father moaning and groaning for his cabbage soup. So the mother said to the next eldest little girl, "Go to the goblin's garden, and tell your sister to bring home those cabbage leaves *at once*."

And the little girl ran off.

The little girl ran into the goblin's garden, calling for her sister. And when she saw the little basket lying among the cabbage plants, and no sister there, she began to call all the louder. She was crying now, too.

And the goblin looked out of a window and shouted, "What are you crying for?"

"My sister," sobbed the little girl. "I can't find my sister!"

"Your sister is looking round the house," said the goblin. "Come up, you'll find her in one of the rooms. You may open all the doors except one door, and that's the one at the top of the little winding staircase. Stop crying now; I've got something pretty for you."

So the little girl went into the house, and the goblin gave her a silver ball. Then she began looking through the rooms, and though she saw many pretty things, she didn't see her sister. And she was coming down into the hall again when she caught sight of the little winding staircase, with the door at the top of it.

"If my sister isn't anywhere else, she must be in the room inside that door," she thought. And she ran quickly up the winding staircase, came to the door at the top, and pulled it open.

Bah! What a dirty, smelly cupboard! No, wherever her sister was, she couldn't be in there! So the little girl tried to shut the cupboard door again, and it stuck; and whilst she was tugging at it, she dropped her silver ball in the slimy mud on the edge of the cupboard floor – and there it was all dirty. The little girl picked it up and rubbed it with her apron. She rubbed, and it got dirtier. She rubbed, she rubbed, she rubbed – the ball got dirtier and dirtier and dirtier. So, having managed at last to shut the cupboard door, she put the ball in her pocket and ran down into the hall.

There was the goblin waiting for her by the front door.

"Where's that silver ball I gave you?"

"Safe in my pocket," said the little girl.

"I don't believe you," said the goblin. "Let me see it!"

The little girl didn't want to let the goblin see her ball. But the goblin was looking angry and she was frightened. So she took the ball out of her pocket – and there it was, covered with mud.

"Ah, you dirty, disobedient child!" screamed the goblin. And he took her by the hair, dragged her up the winding staircase, wrenched open the cupboard door, and threw her, *plump*, down into the pit.

So when neither of the little girls came home the mother began to cry, and the father began to moan, and the mother said to the youngest little girl, "Run, run quickly to the goblin's garden, and bid your sisters come, for I can't think what they can be doing!"

So the youngest little girl ran off to the goblin's garden. And she saw the little basket lying among the cabbage plants, but she didn't see her sisters. So she ran about the garden calling them.

And the goblin put his head out of a window and called down, "What are you making all that noise for?"

"My sisters," said the little girl. "I can't find them. Where are they?"

"Your sisters are looking through the rooms of my house," said the goblin. "And there are so many pretty things to see that they won't be out in a hurry. Come in and go through the rooms yourself. You'll find them in one place or another."

The little girl went into the house then, and the goblin gave her a silver ball. "That's to remember me by," said he, and he went away. But before he went he told her not to open the door at the top of the little winding staircase.

The little girl ran from one room to another; she didn't stop to look at any of the pretty things, she was calling and calling to her sisters. But of course she couldn't find them. And when she had looked through all the rooms, she thought of the door at the top of the winding staircase, and she said to herself, "Well then, my sisters must be in there."

So she ran up the winding staircase and tried to lift the latch of the door. But it was stiff; the door wouldn't open. So she put down her silver ball at the head of the staircase, and put both hands to the latch, and pulled and pushed till the latch lifted and the door came open.

Bah! Only a dirty, smelly cupboard! And what a horrid, slimy pit! But what did she hear? A whimpering and a sobbing rising up from that horrid slimy pit: "Ooo-hu! Ooo-hu!"

"Who's down there?" cried the little girl.

"Ooo-hu! Ooo-hu! We are two little girls. The goblin took us by the hair and flung us down here because we dirtied our silver balls. Ooo-hu! Ooo-hu!"

Then the little girl knew that her sisters were down there, and she leant over the slimy pit and whispered, "Wait a little! I'll get you up!"

And she came out of the cupboard, shut the door, picked up her silver ball, and ran down the winding staircase into the hall.

There was the goblin waiting for her inside the front door.

"What have you done with your silver ball?"

"I have it safe in my two hands."

"Open your hand's and let me see it."

The little girl opened her hands. There was the silver ball lying between her palms, all bright and shining.

"Bravo! Bravo!" cried the goblin. "I love you with all my heart! You shall stay and keep house for me!"

"But – but – Mamma is crying, and Papa is groaning. I must take the cabbage leaves home."

"Well, take them, but promise to come back."

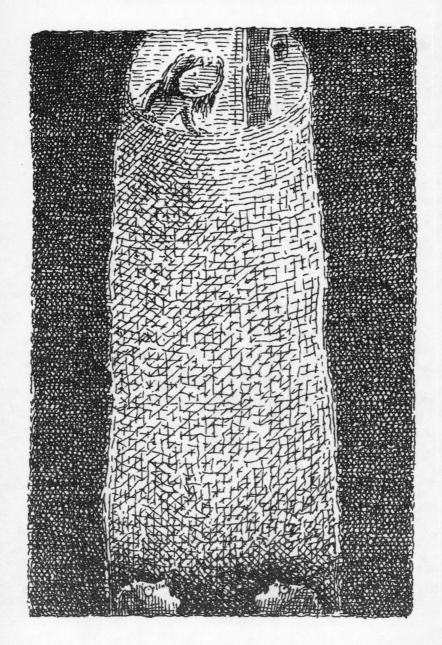

"Yes, I will do that," said the little girl. For she knew that was her only chance of rescuing her sisters.

The goblin opened the front door for her then, and she ran into the garden, snatched up the little basket of cabbage leaves, ran home, found her mother crying in the kitchen, gave her the basket, said, "Now, I'm going to fetch my sisters," and hurried back to the goblin.

She lived with the goblin for a long time. She had to cook his supper and dust and tidy the rooms for him. And finding her so neat and willing, the goblin took to going out every day and not coming home till evening. So the little girl found a long cord, and let it down into the pit and pulled up her two little sisters. My, what a mess they were in! But she washed them and cleaned them, and put them into the topmost room of the house, where the goblin never went. And every day she carried food up to them.

"You have a big appetite," said the goblin, wondering at the way the food disappeared.

"That's because I work so hard," said the little girl.

"Well, I'm not complaining," said the goblin.

So, after she had been with him for some time, that goblin came in one evening, dancing and singing.

"You don't know," said he, "you don't know! But I shall never die!"

The little girl felt bad when she heard that, but she managed to smile.

"That's good news then!" said she. "And how does that come about?"

"Because my soul is inside an eggshell," grinned the goblin.

"Oh, that's splendid!" said the little girl.

"Yes," said the goblin, "I shall never die unless the eggshell gets dirty or broken. And I shall take good care that never happens!"

"Well, look after yourself!" said the little girl.

But next evening, when the goblin came home, she put on a sad, sad face. She kept sighing and doing her best to cry. And, no – she wouldn't eat anything!

"What's the matter now?" said the goblin.

"Oh, oh, you told me you would never die. But if dirt gets into the egg, the dirt would kill you. Let me see the egg, let me see if it is dirty or clean! Oh, I *must* see it! Then if it is all clean, I shall be happy again!"

"Ah, ah!" said the goblin. "You would betray me?"

"*I* betray you!" said the little girl. "Aren't I your good little servant?"

Well, at first the goblin wouldn't show her the egg; but she bothered so, and cried so, that at last he brought it out of his pocket. But he held it in his hand and wouldn't let her touch it.

"There," said he, "you see it's as clean as a new pin!"

"Is it as clean as a new pin?" said the little girl. "Look – what's that? Isn't that a tiny speck of dirt?"

"Where?" said the goblin.

"Just there," said the little girl.

"I can't see any dirt!" said the goblin.

"There, there, surely you must see it!" said the little girl. And she struck the egg with the palm of her hand. The egg fell to the floor and broke: the goblin gave a great yell and toppled over, stone dead.

The little girl ran upstairs to her sisters. "Come out! Come down!" she called. "The goblin is dead and we are free!"

Down came the two sisters, laughing and shouting.

They carried the dead goblin out into the garden, dug a hole and buried him. And it wasn't a big hole they had to dig, because he was so small. So they soon had the earth over him. Then they took the keys, locked up the house, and ran home.

The father was still lying in his bed, moaning and groaning. But when he saw his three little daughters come in, he jumped up and dressed himself. No, he wasn't ill any more! As for the mother, she went on shedding tears, but now they were tears of happiness. They all hurried to the goblin's house, and in the cellar they found a great heap of treasure. And since there was no one to claim that treasure, they took it for themselves. Now they were rich. They built themselves a fine big house in the goblin's garden.

But the father pulled down the goblin's old house, because he said that a place where such things happened was best out of sight and out of mind.

LOST – ONE PAIR OF LEGS

Joan Aiken

*O*nce there was a vain, proud, careless, thoughtless boy called Cal Finhorn, who was very good at tennis. He won this game, he won that game, he won this match, he won that match, and then he won a tournament, and had a silver cup with his name on it.

Winning this cup made him even prouder – too proud to speak to any of the other players at the tournament. As soon as he could, he took his silver cup and hurried away to the entrance of the sports ground, where the buses stop.

"Just wait till I show them this cup at home," he was thinking. "I'll make Jenny polish it every day."

Jenny was Cal's younger sister. He made her do lots of things for him – wash his cereal bowl, make his bed, clean his shoes, feed his rabbits.

He had not allowed her to come to the tournament, in case he lost.

On the way across the grass towards the bus stop, Cal saw a great velvety fluttering butterfly with purple and white and black circles on its wings.

Cal was a boy who acted before he thought. Maybe sometimes he didn't think at all. He hit the butterfly a smack with his tennis racket, and it fell to the ground, stunned. Cal felt sorry then, perhaps, for what he had done to it, but it was too late, for he heard a tremendous clap of thunder and then he saw the Lady Esclairmonde, the queen of winged things, hovering right in his path.

She looked very frightening indeed – she was all wrapped in a cloak of grey and white feathers, she had the face of a hawk, hands like claws, a crest of flame, and her hair and ribbons and the train of her dress flew out sideways, as if a force twelve gale surrounded her. Cal could hear a fluttering sound, such as a flag or sail makes in a high wind. His own heart was fluttering inside him; he could hear that too, like a lark inside a biscuit tin.

"Why did you hit my butterfly, Cal?" asked the Lady Esclairmonde.

Cal tried to brazen it out. He grinned at the lady. But he glanced nervously round him, wondering if people noticed that she was speaking to him. Perhaps, he thought hopefully, they might think she was congratulating him on his silver cup.

Nobody else seemed to have noticed the lady.

"Ah, shucks, it was only a silly butterfly," said Cal. "Anyway I don't suppose I hurt it."

"Oh," said the lady. "What makes you think that?"

"It hasn't written me a letter of complaint," said Cal, grinning.

As he spoke these words he noticed a very odd feeling under his right hip. And when he looked down, he saw his right leg remove itself from him, and go hopping off across the grass, heel and toe, heel and toe, as if it were dancing a hornpipe. The leg seemed delighted to be off and away on its own. It went dancing over to the bus stop. Just then a number 19 bus swept in to the stop, and the leg hopped up on board and was borne way.

"*Hey!*" bawled Cal in horror. "Come back! Come back! You're my leg! You've no right to go off and leave me in the lurch. And that isn't the right bus!"

Lurch was the right word. With only one leg, Cal was swaying about like a hollyhock in a gale. He was obliged to prop himself up with his tennis racket. He turned angrily to the lady and said, "Did *you* do that? You've no right to take away my leg! It isn't fair!"

"Nothing is fair," said the lady sternly. "What you did to my butterfly was not fair either. You may think yourself lucky I didn't take the other leg as well."

"I think you are a mean old witch!" said Cal.

Instantly he felt a jerk as his left leg undid itself from the hip. Cal bumped down on to the grass, hard, while his left leg went capering away across the grass, free as you please, up on the point of its toe, pirouetting like a ballerina. When it reached the bus stop a number 16 had just pulled up; the left leg hopped nimbly on board and was carried away.

"You're on the wrong bus! Come back!" shouted Cal, but the leg made no answer to that.

Tod Crossfinch, who was in Cal's class at school, came by just then.

"Coo! Cal," he said, "you lost your legs, then?"

"You can blooming well see I have!" said Cal angrily.

"Want me to wheel you to the bus stop in my bike basket?" said Tod.

"No! I want my legs back," said Cal.

"You won't get them back," the Lady Esclairmonde told him, "until a pair of butterflies brings them."

Then she vanished in a flash of lightning and a smell of burnt feathers.

"Who was that?" said Tod. "Was that the new French teacher? You sure you don't want me to wheel you as far as the bus stop, Cal?"

"Oh, all right," said Cal, very annoyed; so Tod packed him in his bike basket and wheeled him to the stop, and then waited and helped him on to a number 2 bus. It was all very upsetting and embarrassing. People on the bus said, "Ooh, look! There's a boy whose legs have gone off and left him. He *must* have treated them badly. Wonder what he did?"

When Cal got to his own stop the conductor had to lift him off the bus, and then he had to walk into the garden on his hands. Luckily he was quite good at that. There he found his sister Jenny feeding her butterflies. She had about forty tame ones who used to come every day when she sprinkled sugar on a tray: small blue ones, large white ones, yellow ones, red-and-black ones, and big beautiful tortoiseshells, peacocks, red admirals, and purple emperors. They were flittering and fluttering all around Jenny, with a sound like falling leaves.

"Ooh, Cal," said Jenny; "*whatever* have you done with your legs?"

"They ran off and left me," said Cal, very annoyed that he had to keep telling people that his legs didn't want to stay with him.

As Cal spoke, all the butterflies rose up in a cloud of wings and flew away.

"Oh, poor Cal!" said Jenny. "Never mind, I'll wheel you about in my doll's pushchair."

"I'd rather wheel myself about on your skate-

board," said Cal.

Jenny was rather disappointed, but she kindly let him have the skateboard.

"Er, Jenny," said Cal, "you don't suppose your butterflies would bring back my legs, do you?"

"Oh, no, Cal," said Jenny. "Why should they? You haven't done anything for them. In fact they don't like you much, because you always chase them and try to catch them in your handkerchief."

Cal's father said that Cal had better try advertising to get his legs back.

So he put a card in the post office window, and also a notice in the local paper:

LOST

One pair of legs. Reward offered.

Lots and lots of people turned up hoping for the reward, but the legs they brought were never the right ones. There were old, rheumatic legs in wrinkled boots, or skinny girls' legs in knitted legwarmers, or babies' legs or football legs or ballet dancers' legs in pink cotton slippers.

"I never knew before that so many legs ran

away from their owners," said Jenny.

This fact ought to have cheered Cal up a bit, but it didn't.

Jenny would have liked to adopt a pair of the ballet legs, but her mother said no, a canary and some rabbits were all the pets they had room for. "Besides, those legs must belong to someone else who wants them back."

Then a friend told Cal's father that one of Cal's legs was performing every night in the local pub, the Ring o' Roses. "Dances around on the bar, very active, it does. Brings in a whole lot o' custom."

Mr Finhorn went along one night to see, and sure enough he recognised Cal's leg, with the scar on the knee where he had fallen down the front steps carrying a bottle of milk. But when the leg saw Mr Finhorn it danced away along the bar, and skipped out of the window, and went hopping off down the road in the dark.

The other leg was heard of up in London; it had got a job at the Hippodrome Theatre, dancing on the stage with a parasol tucked into its garter.

"I don't believe they'll *ever* come back to me now," said Cal hopelessly.

Cal was becoming very sad and quiet, not a bit like what he had been before. He was a good deal nicer to Jenny and even helped his mother with the dishwashing, balancing on a kitchen stool.

"It's not very likely," his mother agreed. "Not now they're used to earning their own living."

"Maybe if you fed my butterflies every day, they'd bring your legs back," suggested Jenny.

So Cal rolled out on his skateboard every day and fed the butterflies with handfuls of sugar. They grew quite accustomed to him, and would perch on his arms and head and hands.

But summer was nearly over; autumn was coming; there were fewer butterflies every day. And still Cal's legs did not come back.

School began again. Every day Cal went to school on the skateboard, rolling himself along with his hands. He couldn't play football, because of having no legs, but he could still swim, so he did that three times a week in the school pool.

One day while he was swimming he saw two butterflies floating in the centre of the pool. They were flapping and struggling a little, but very feebly; it looked as if they were going to drown.

Cal dog-paddled towards them, as far as he could. "Poor things," he thought, "they must feel horrible with their wings all wet and floppy."

They were two of a kind he had never seen before – very large, silvery in colour, with lavender streaks and long trailing points to their wings.

Cal wondered how he could save them.

"For if I take them in my hands," he thought, "I might squash them. And they would have to go under water when I swim. Oh, if only I had my legs! Then I could swim with my legs and hold the butterflies above water."

But he hadn't got his legs, so he could only swim with his arms.

"I'll have to take the butterflies in my mouth," Cal thought then.

He didn't much care for the idea. In fact it made him shivery down his back – to think of having two live, fluttery butterflies inside his mouth. Still, that seemed the only way to save them. He opened his mouth very wide indeed – luckily it was a big one anyway – and gently scooped the two butterflies in with his tongue, as they themselves scoop in sugar. He was careful to take in as little water as possible.

Then, with open mouth and head well above water, he swam like mad for the side of the pool.

But, on the way, the butterflies began to fidget and flutter inside his mouth.

"Oh, I can't bear it," thought Cal.

Now the butterflies were beating and battering inside his mouth – he felt as if his head were hollow, and the whole of it were filled with great flapping wings and kicking legs and waving whiskers. They tickled and rustled and scraped and scrabbled and nearly drove him frantic. Still he went on swimming as fast as he was able.

Then it got so bad that he felt as if his whole head were going to be lifted off. But it was not only his head – suddenly Cal, head, arms, and all, found himself lifted right out of the swimming pool and carried through the air by the two butterflies whirring like helicopters inside his mouth.

They carried him away from the school and back to his own garden, full of lavender and nasturtiums and Michaelmas daisies, where Jenny was scattering sugar on a tray.

And there, sitting in a deck chair waiting for him, were his own two legs!

Cal opened his mouth so wide in amazement that the two silvery butterflies shot out, and dropped down onto the tray to refresh themselves with a little sugar. Which they must have needed, after carrying Cal all wet and dripping.

And Cal's legs stood up, stretched themselves a bit, in a carefree way, heel and toe, the way cats do, then came hopping over to hook themselves on to Cal's hips, as calm and friendly as if they had never been away.

Was Cal a different boy after that? He was indeed. For one thing, those legs had learnt such a lot while they were off on their own that he could have made an easy living in any circus, or football team, or dance company – and did, for a while, when he grew up.

Also, he never grew tired of listening to his legs, who used to argue in bed, every night, recalling the days when they had been off in the world by themselves.

". . . That time when I jumped into the tiger's

cage. . ."

"Shucks! That wasn't so extra brave. Not like when I tripped up the bank robbers. . ."

"That was nothing."

"You weren't there. You don't know how it happened!"

So they used to argue.

For the rest of his life Cal was very polite to his legs, in case they ever took a fancy to go off on holiday again.

THE GIRL WHO MARRIED A PIXIE

Alison Uttley

A poor labourer once lived in a small thatched cottage on the edge of Dartmoor. There he took his wife when they were married and there all the children were born. Fourteen of them, and all as bonny as the little flowers that grow among the grasses! Their laughter and merriment kept his heart from failing, and gave strength to his hands, but he was hard-pressed for money to buy them food, and many a day they went short. The prettiest of all the brood was the eldest, Polly, with her long golden hair and blue eyes. She helped her mother all day with never a frown or grumble, and carried the babies out to the moor, where she sat knitting as she watched over them. It was there the pixie must have seen her.

One night it rained in torrents, and the wind beat on the cottage and blew wildly round the corners of the little building, screaming and crying as if it wanted to come in and join the children inside. The cottage was warm and cosy, for there was a red fire of wood, and the family sat round the hearth playing dominoes on the trestle board.

Suddenly there was a tap-tap-tap at the door. The laughter of the children ceased, and the mother put her finger on her lips and listened. The father took a cudgel and went to see who it was, for in those days robbers walked on Dartmoor.

He opened the door a crack and looked out, but he could see nobody. Then something brushed past his legs, and in rode a pixie, no bigger than a hand's span. His steed was a heather broom, and in his hand he carried a whip of rushes.

"Good evening to you," said the little man, sweeping off his green hat with a fine bow, and standing by his broom horse, holding it by its bridle.

"Good evening, sir," replied the labourer, and the children stared with wide eyes, and even the baby forgot to whimper and chuckled at the funny little man in his fine clothes.

"Will you give me your eldest daughter to wed?" asked the pixie, without more delay, as if he hadn't a moment so spare. "I'll give you as much gold as you like."

"Certainly not," cried the labourer; and his wife said:

"I should think not, indeed. Let our Polly marry a pixie? No! Never!" She put her arm round Polly's waist, and the children all ran round their sister and held tightly to her skirts.

The pixie was quite prepared for this refusal, but he called aloud in a strange tongue and the door flew open. In came another pixie bearing a pot of gold, all shining yellow as buttercups.

"All this for you, and many a pot like it, if you'll give me your eldest daughter. I've watched her on the moors and I love her and would marry her."

"No!" cried Polly's mother. "Never! Upon my word, what are things coming to? Off you go, little man, and don't darken my doorway again."

She flapped her apron at the two pixies as if they had been hens and away they went, one dragging the gold, the other riding his steed of heather.

You may be sure the family talked of nothing else that night but the pixies' visit, and they told one another that never would they let their dear Polly go. Then Polly got the supper of roast potatoes and goats' milk, and put the children to bed. She climbed in beside her sisters and lay thinking of the pixie. Nobody had asked her whether she wanted to marry him. Indeed, only the baker's boy had ever asked to marry her, and her heart beat as she thought of this strange happening.

Then she heard her parents whispering together. "If we had that gold we could buy our cottage, and the field and the orchard beyond, and live here, rich as rich, with apple trees and sheep and a cow," her father murmured.

"I could buy new clothes for all the children,

and give them food every day, so that they would grow up strong and well," said the mother.

Then they both said, "But to marry a pixie! No! We won't let our darling Polly marry a pixie! Not for all the riches in the world will we allow it."

The next night it was even stormier and the wind cried and howled round the house, shaking and banging the walls. The children sat with their parents, and they spoke of the fierceness of the gale. Suddenly there was a tap-tap-tap at the door.

"The pixie," they all whispered, and the father went to the door and opened it a crack.

In rode the pixie again, and the heather broom pranced and kicked and snorted.

"Good evening to you," said the little man, and he swept off his hat politely and stood waiting in the middle of the floor.

"Good evening, sir," replied the labourer, and the children all came round to watch for they had no fear of the little man.

"Will you give me your eldest daughter to wed?" asked the pixie, calmly, as if he had never asked such a thing before. "I'll give you a saucepan that will never be empty."

"Certainly not," cried the labourer indignantly. "I told you before, sir, that we can't part with Polly."

The pixie gave a whistle, shrill as a bird's call, and the door flew open. In came another pixie bearing a saucepan, dark and streaked with green, an ancient pot of bronze.

The pixie put it on the floor and said something. Into the pan flew a cock pheasant, and sat there content.

He spoke again, and a piglet wriggled and squealed in the saucepan.

Again he spoke and a plum pudding all hot and sweet-smelling simmered there.

The children's eyes nearly popped out of their heads and they shrieked with excitement as the pixie held out the saucepan to their father.

"All this for you, and another pot like it, if you'll give me your eldest daughter. I've watched her on the hills and I love her and would marry her."

"Never! Never!" cried the parents, and away went the pixies without another word.

Now the maiden's eyes had been fixed upon the pixie, and she saw something she liked. His small wee face was kind, although it was wrinkled like a walnut. His smile was merry, and the glance he cast on her was full of love.

"Why shouldn't I marry him?" she said to herself. "I was gong to marry the baker's boy, but he whips his horse cruel hard, and he might whip me. The pixie carried a whip, but he never used it to that broomstick nag of his. I think he'd be a better husband than the baker's boy."

So when the pixie came the third time, riding into the house on a wilder night than ever, carrying a musical box which would play every tune in the world, she up and spoke.

"Father and Mother dear! I've a mind to wed the pixie," said she. "If he brings you the pot of gold, and the never-empty saucepan, and the musical box which will play every tune, then I will wed him."

The pixie clapped his little hands and in came other pixies with the gifts. The father and mother protested and wept, but Polly's mind was made up. She slipped into her bedroom and made up her clothes in a bundle, her Sunday dress, her best shoes, her aprons, and she followed the little fellow out into the night.

"Climb up behind me, dear heart," said the

pixie, and she sat on the heather broom and put her thumbs on his slender strong waist.

Up they rose in the air, whirling through the wind over the dark moor till they came to the group of black rocks called Honey Bag Tor. On the face of the greatest rock the pixie knocked three times, and the side of the stone opened. The girl stared up at the sky and round at the cowering wild ponies sheltering by the tor, their eyes wide, their nostrils quivering, for they knew one of the little people was near them.

"Come along to your new home, Polly dear," said the pixie, and he tenderly took her hand and led her inside the darkness of the rock. Down and down they went to the great rooms, warmed by earth-heat, lighted by luminous stones decorated with flowers made out of gold and precious stones, the work of the little men. Pixies, you should know, have carved and cut the gems of the underworld for long ages, ever since man displaced them on the green earth and sent them to their own land, and they are skilful and clever beyond human knowledge.

In the vast hall many tables were spread for the wedding feast, and the young girl walked proudly down the room by the side of the little

man to her seat.

"She's here! She's come at last! The human girl has come!" cried the pixies and a thousand guests waved their hands and came swarming out of the many passages chattering in a strange tongue, and clambering to their tiny chairs.

There was honey in gold dishes, and Devonshire cream in crystal bowls. There was sweet bread made from the yellow wheat of the cornfields, and wine from the heather-bells. The girl Polly ate the good food and drank the scented heather-wine, for she was hungry after the wild ride across the moor.

"What a tale I'll have to tell them when I go home," she thought. "Won't Father be surprised! And Mother, too! My sisters and brothers will like to hear of this fine feast. Perhaps the pixie will let me take some strawberries and peaches."

In those warm lands deep in the earth grew fruits and flowers of tropical countries, and Polly tasted and enjoyed things she had never met before.

Then came an ancient pixie, as old as the hills, with a beard sweeping the ground. He married her to her lover, and bound her finger with a ring of grasses.

Even as the old manikin spoke the words of wisdom over her, she grew smaller, till she was only as big as the pixies themselves. Then she was taken to her room, a blue and silver bedroom, and the bed was covered with silk sheets and lamb's wool blankets. Hanging behind woven tapestries were dresses fine as cobwebs, and chests of jewels and clothes rich and rare, all made ready for the pixie bride. Polly took off her country clothes, which were shrunken and queer like the withered leaves of last year. Her little bundle was not needed, her Sunday dress was a blue tattered rag and she looked at it in wonder. Already her memory was changed. Once she had worn that dress, and those old shoes and stockings. Somebody had blessed her and kissed her, someone far away. She put on the tiny linen nightgown laid out on her bed ready for her, and brushed her shining hair. Then she got into bed and slept. How long she was asleep I cannot tell you, but when she awoke she remembered nothing of her past life.

The pixie husband was kind and loving, and she was happy with him. In time she bore him a son, and then a daughter, and the little half-human children had great beauty. They played in the rock's interior, and ran shouting down the bright corridors deep in the earth. But when the moon was full they came through the stone door and rode their heather brooms on the purple moorland, or they clung to the manes of the Dartmoor ponies and were carried shrieking and laughing, as they kicked their small heels against the animals' necks, across the valleys and over the hills of the moor. Polly had forgotten that outside world, and even when she stepped on the heather, a tiny creature in her green dress, no memory came of the life she had once lived there.

When the two children were nine or ten years old by pixie reckoning, Polly suddenly remembered her father and mother and the cottage where she was born, and the reason she thought of them was this. Her young children came running home dragging a baby's slipper which they had found on the tor, dropped by some mother from her infant's foot. Polly turned it over, wondering why it stirred some vague memory in her mind. Then she saw her own mother with the happy brood of children in the thatched cottage, and herself with the baby, sitting on the moor. The memory of hoe came flooding over her with such force she couldn't resist it. She went to her pixie husband and said to him:

"My dear one, I have just remembered my home, the cottage where my mother and father live, and all the little ones. I remember the hearthstone, and the potatoes roasting in the open fire, and the sticks crackling in the chimney. Let me go and visit them."

"Don't go, beloved," implored the pixie. "This is your home. One can never retrace one's steps."

"Oh let me go! I must tell them about my own children," she cried, clutching his arm. "I must kiss them all, for I love them."

So he took her by the hand and led her out of the great door in the rock, and gave her a drink of the pale wine which she had tasted at her wedding feast. She grew tall once more, and she walked over the moorland tracks, past the great tors, walking many a mile, breathing the cold pure air, stepping so lightly over the heather that her feet scarcely bent the purple flowers. Sometimes she ran, and her long golden hair flew like wings behind her. Animals and birds had no fear of her, for she made no sound as she sped by.

At last she came to the little valley she knew so well, to the stream where she had paddled, and the rocks where she had nursed her sisters and brothers. She turned the corner, and stopped bewildered. Where the cottage used to stand was a great house, with strange horseless carriages, black and shining as giant beetles, rolling in and out of a broad drive, hooting and shrieking like owls and night birds.

She stood very still, listening, staring, not daring to venture near. Then she saw an old man coming up the hill, carrying a basket of mushrooms, and she stepped over the grass on her bare feet and held out her white arms to him.

"Please will you tell me where Primrose Cottage is? I thought it was here. I am sure it was here," she asked, and her voice had the music of fairy people in it.

"I've never heard of it," he replied slowly, staring at her long, straight, green dress, and the gold hair hanging like a cloak around her.

"But this is the place. I remember. There is

the gate, and the field where I used to play. What is that house?"

"It's the Grand Hotel," replied the old man. "I've heard my grandfather say that once upon a time there stood a cottage and garden there, but that was over a hundred years ago, and this hotel is for folk to come to the moor and get the fresh air.

"Where might ye be from?" he asked as the lady did not move.

She shook her head and turned slowly away, and as he looked after her he saw that her white feet moved over the grass without leaving any prints, and the flowers remained upright as she passed.

"I've seen a pixie, I'm certain sure," said old George at the inn that night. "I could tell she was one of them by the colour of her long hair, and the way she walked, light as a fairy."

"You should have held fast to her skirts, and not let her go till she gave you your wish," said his friends, mocking him.

"Nay, she was crying, fit to break her heart. I felt mortal sorry for her," he replied.

"Then she was no pixie, for they feel neither sorrow nor pain," said another.

"I tell ye, she was a pixie, I'm certain sure, and she stood looking at the hotel, and talking about some cottage or other."

"There's a tale of a girl who lived there once, on the moor's edge. She went off with the pixie folk, and was never heard of again. Clean disappeared off the face of the earth, they say, and her mother and father mourned all their lives, rich as they were. The children went away and lived over Exeter, but the parents looked for her always, and stayed here on the moor, waiting for her to come back."

It was an ancient man in the corner who spoke, and some said by his queer ways he was a relation of that pixie-led girl.

"Then I've seen her. That was who she was. She'd come back to find her home. Come back and everyone gone," said old George, and he called for a pot of ale, and drank to try to forget the girl's grief.

At the stone doorway of Honey Bag Tor waited the green pixie man. In his hand he had the cup of forgetfulness, for he knew that his wife would only find sorrow when she walked the moor again. Then he saw his dear one, wandering with her head bent, her step wavering and lost, as she fell in the bogs and stumbled over the rocks. Her tears were bringing back her mortality, and she felt all the griefs and troubles of mankind, nor could she find the way to the pixie folk or remember the life she had led with them.

He ran to meet her, crying, "Dear wife! Beloved Polly! How we have missed you! How we have longed for your return! The children are calling for you. Come, drink and forget again."

"Nobody was there," she sobbed. "It was a hundred years ago they lived. All was changed, and the cottage gone, and they dead. A hundred years! How can it be when I am young and beautiful?"

"Time doesn't exist for the pixie folk. We live outside it, and it has no power over us. Drink this, sweet wife. Drink and then come down to your home and your children."

She drank deep of the draught in the crystal cup and forgetfulness entered her mind, and immortality caught her up. She became small in stature and gay-hearted, and her sorrows slipped away from her.

Laughing gaily she ran down the rock's

hidden ways to the little children and played
with them through the enchanted days, and her
husband loved her dearly. Yet sometimes a dim
memory came to her, a faint remembrance of
earth people, living their own human lives with
their children. Then she took some small toy or
treasure and threw it into the heather or laid it
on the dark rocks for the earth children to find.

So if you ever discover a tiny carved manikin
made from a bone, or a pebble of gold, or a
necklace of dewdrops like opals, you will know
it is a gift from Polly, who was once a girl like
you.

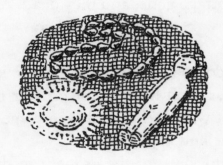

ACKNOWLEDGEMENTS

The editor and publishers gratefully acknowledge the following for permission to reproduce copyright material in this anthology:

A. M. Heath and Company Ltd for 'Lost – One Pair of Legs' by Joan Aiken from *The Last Slice of Rainbow*, copyright © Joan Aiken 1985; Susan Dickinson for 'The King of the Cats', copyright © Susan Dickinson 1996; Penguin Books Ltd for 'The Old White Ghost and the Old Grey Granddad' by Dorothy Edwards from *The Magician Who Kept a Pub*, Viking Children's Books, copyright © Dorothy Edwards 1975; David Higham Associates for 'The Sea-Baby' by Eleanor Farjeon from *The Old Nurse's Stocking Basket*, Oxford University Press, 1931; also for 'The Three Silver Balls' by Ruth Manning-Sanders from *A Book of Ghosts and Goblins*, Methuen & Co, copyright © Ruth Manning-Sanders 1968; HarperCollins*Publishers* Ltd for 'The Legend of Alderley' by Alan Garner from *The Weirdstone of Brisingamen*, copyright © Alan Garner 1960; Laura Cecil Literary Agency for 'A Cloak for Amanita' by Adèle Geras, first published in Cricket Magazine 1976, copyright © Adèle Geras 1976, 1977; also for 'The Odd Glove' by Philippa Pearce, copyright © Philippa Pearce 1996; Pavilion Books Ltd for 'The Wonderful Cake-Horse' by Terry Jones, copyright © Terry Jones 1981; The Orion Publishing Group Ltd for 'The Thief and the Magic' by Margaret Mahy from *The Second Margaret Mahy Storybook*, J. M. Dent, copyright Margaret Mahy; Faber and Faber Ltd for 'The Girl Who Married a Pixie' by Alison Uttley from *Mustard, Pepper and Salt* by Alison Uttley.